The Purple Lady...

The Purple Lady...

JITESH

PARTRIDGE

To order additional copies of this book, contact
Partridge India
000 800 10062 62
orders.india@partridgepublishing.com

www.partridgepublishing.com/india

Contents

Yes, like every other author I also tried to write a book, but it would have been a difficult task to complete the book without help of certain people. I would like to thank all those who helped me in writing the book.

First of all, I would like to thank my family (Ma, Papa, Sister and Brother-in-Law) who gave me freedom to come up with something, which was my dream.

Secondly, I am thankful to Raja Mohanty Sir who helped me in editing the book by providing his precious time. He also gave me true and fruitful reviews on my book. He was my faculty during graduation at Rourkela Institute of Management Studies, Odisha.

I would also like to thank Manish Singha for designing the cover page of the book.

Next, I would like to thank people, some are my friends and others were just passersby's. They unknowingly helped me by narrating their love stories and experiences of life, which helped me to tie a knot and club them to make a story.

I am also thankful to few friends like Manpreet Singh, Parag Parekh, Hritvick Sen, Vivek Sharma, Kishor Joshi, Surendra Pandey and a few more, who kept poking me by questioning what about your book and when they will get a chance to buy it.

Prologue

This is the story of a girl whose simplicity is her uniqueness. She is completely entwined with the mundane of daily life of her family. She is torn between sudden rushes of excitements and sweeping depressions. And what adds to her woes is her impulsive nature and for that the way, bang on, she lands into trouble time and again. The little I have understood her is her patented strength to the word 'mishap' with all its manifestations included. And above all her vulnerability lies in her gullibility, but for me that is charm and beauty to say.

And with this little description, let's begin with the story of "The Purple Lady".

Synopsis

The Purple Lady is the story of the girl who is vividly narcissist, a struggler and of course someone who had promised life that she would not be enjoying it at a constant pace. The best part of her story is that random incidences are a part and parcel of her life. Unlike the Ravanna of yore, who possessed the elixir of life in his belly, she possessed the figurative gem of eternal conflict in hers.

Amid the tragedies of life and the sadness that kept her tripping almost everywhere, she meets a person who promises to take away all her worries and was ready to share her all pains for rest of the life.

The story started with trust, they become friends and finally in love. And they became victims of this infection. Problems, they kept coming in different intervals keeping pace with her journey of life. For example – she gets diagnosed with a cancerous cyst in her ovaries and this would not allow her to conceive. This is just to name one, and the person who came into her life ignored along with other more ailments. The story holds a lot of incidents that burnish the trust the duo had in each other, and it also reveals the pain that broke apart the budding relationship and finally tore it asunder.

So, a stereotypical Brahmin youth from Bihar named Kanisk falls for a beautiful Sikh girl. Or was it the otherwise, girl catching the wrong end of the callow Bihari youth, Kanisk. The discussions and decisions, challenges and the love trials, everything will just remind of love, sniffles and rejuvenation. Carry on!

You are most open to God, when your heart is wide open, and your mind is settled and worry-free. For most of us, this happens in the presence of our beloved --- Anonymous

When Kanisk saw her for the first time

There are times in a city-dwellers' life when he beholds the majesty of the Himalayas and realises that this mountain range is the Zeus of eponymous 'high-rises'. I'm in Dehradun, the capital of Uttarakhand, and it was a beautiful morning on the foothills of lower Himalayan ranges (Shivalik).

I stood outside my bedroom balcony, savouring every moment as I soaked in the morning sun rising from the heart of the mountains, creating a rainbow and painting me and the city with its colour and warmth. The day was 5th November, 2010. And it was, the first dawn in the city of Dehradun for me. The important historical agonies of my own life, all the regrets and past baggage seemed to me fading away in the distant mighty Himalaya with the new beginning. (I had visited Dehradun before; it was a hurried afternoon pit-stop!). Now, at 8 o' clock in the morning, on the first day in the city, I was experiencing excitement at the prospect of expected new beginning which I was in probability waiting for.

I was motivated with the challengingly mysterious day ahead of me. It was the new job in hand. That day my feeling was the world would kneel before my spirit!

Well let me take short personal break to introduce myself, so there...

I am Kanisk.

A few days back, my company promoted me as in-charge of its placement and Content Head. I have two tasks in my hand. First is to identify and recruit candidates for the content project for my company through campus recruitment. And the second one is to set up a complete new branch of the firm at Dehradun. Besides, my other job here entails to make the new recruits to learn the art of writing. And above all I am also responsible for managing company's operations here, so I expected a long stay in the offing.

And I conducted innumerable campus drives met several new, young faces. But, there was one, who didn't even bother to appear for the test conducted by our company, but appeared directly for the interview. Of course she was the direct fall out of nepotism. The girl being the daughter of someone in the institute, where the placement was conducted, she came at the time when we were getting ready to declare the final result for selection and then wrap of the day. However, we had no choice but to entertain this girl. We allowed her some time to settle down as she was sweating despite the winter chill settling in. And she completely confused me. Her answers confused me and I first tried to figure out whether she really wanted this job or had to bow before the diktat of someone mighty in her closer surrounding.

The Purple Lady...

As her selection was preordained so we took little time recruit her and declared the result. The result brought happiness to many when we looked at the beaming faces of those who got selected but, I was not surprised her pale her face despite getting the nod from us. She was the Lady in Purple or the leading lady of this story, the Purple Lady.

You would want to know the reason for calling her so. But to know this, you will have to wait a while.

A deliberate Tadka to the Sloka of Karma

Her letter of intent was handed over to the management of the institute where we conducted our campus drive and moved out. We reached the office by 9:00 pm, and left soon after tending to some minor issues. The next day was Sunday but that was an unofficial working day for us, especially for me being the centre head. I had to finalise issues relating to infrastructure of our new office. And apart from that Sunday our discussions hovered around the new recruits, their expectations, how to groom them at the earliest possible time along with the unpredictable showers of Dehradun. Finally I went on a long biking to Mussorie and came back late in night to my room. I was relaxed as the last couple of days were satisfactory beyond my satisfaction.

The clock was showing 7:30 am, when I woke up. By the time I reached office there was a situation waiting for me and instructions came from my head office to rush back to Delhi. I did that and explained the day's work ahead to my subordinate before leaving.

I came back after two days and got busy with my daily chores at the office. The induction of the new trainees and introduction to the work culture of my organisation, other managerial works and so on. But, I was keeping a close eye on the girl whom we had to recruit under little dilemma from both the sides. I was trying to understand her attitude towards the work, her sense of responsibility, her dealing with fellow trainees and above all her thinking towards organisation and its work culture, which I had explained with all sincerity. But, a shock was waiting for me. After two days in office she simply came to me and asked for a 15 days leave for her sister's marriage, which was supposed to be held at Chandigarh. I am a firm believer of the Karma theory proposed by Lord Krishna in Bhagavad Gita and expect those working for me to adhere to that. So, my first reaction was she was not going to work here anymore after her return.

The days ahead were hectic with the mundane activities like training, more training, updates and more updates, and there was no respite for me. But, amidst all the chaos Purple Lady, who had vanished without even blinking an eye, kept on coming to my mind. No matter how much I tried she was there whenever I was little free.

Her recurrence in my memory was just for nothing. It was not that I was not smitten with her but it was proficiency as a content writer was miles ahead of than the new recruits. This was the reason for which I thought about her and giving her chances and try to understand what was there in her mind. Meanwhile, her time of return was approaching and I was immersed with the project and new assignments and other things in life were out of my mind.

The Period of Challenges

She came back and was completely changed person. She started taking things seriously and as usual she showed much improved skill than other trainees. I did not have to concentrate much on her work because it was not necessary, as she was almost like a professional. I was wondering why and what really brought a complete turnaround in her and the zeal she showed towards her work was really infectious. Things started settling down around this wonderful professional I had hired.

The office atmosphere was fast changing. We were settling things quite fast now. My responsibility along with authority as the team and business head had grown tremendously. It was time for selecting my immediate subordinate to ease me of pressure so that I could concentrate on some more pressing activities. My first choice was of course she as she had already proved her mettle. She was proving as a worth deputy with her professionalism and the speed she showed to learn the nitty-gritty of our business. Her best part was she was showing clock like precision in everything with a human touch.

With responsibility growing I was getting keen on the issue of my immediate subordinate. Despite my inclination to ask her to shoulder more responsibilities I thought it would be prudent to give fair chance to all those deserving in the group of 20. To my utter despair no one really showed any keenness to become my immediate subordinate and share bigger responsibilities with functional authority. Everybody, whom I had in my mind for the position, chickened with flimsy grounds and surprisingly when her chances came she grabbed without any qualm, and frankly I was not surprised.

Given the response of the team and performance I was certain to select her and I did that. Along with that I selected one of her youngest colleague in the group, and this was a big task for both of them. Meanwhile, I informed the entire branch about the development and tried to ease their discomfort at the promotion they were getting at this early part of their career. Finally they agreed for which I had to do a little bit of coaxing and I was happy for that. And this was formally informed to all in the team with little disagreement which finally subsided.

Cries of Bonding

Things, which you may say operations in the office became streamlined and everybody was showing signs of complete settling down. There was a complete harmony and team spirit and for me it was the best part. Meanwhile, my closeness with my immediate subordinates was increasing and especially with Purple Lady. But, one trait of her really amazed me was her ready to drop tears in her eyes. One day I found her crying and my enquiry with her, after a while, revealed that it was a message from her boyfriend, Rishabh.

I never knew that her revelation would be a bit of embarrassment for me. It was 'I' who was being put on the dock by his boyfriend Rishabh. I knew it was immaturity on his part but what he was doing perhaps very natural to him. He had put the entire relationship on a big question mark. He was suspicious towards me and my intention. For Rishabh, the promotion of Purple Lady was entirely based on her closeness, as he believed, to me and it was not her professional competency. For a moment I was at loss of words and was unable to react. It took me sometime to become normal and then I suggested that I should speak to him to which she opposed vehemently. Her only apprehension was this might aggravate the situation and finish the relation. I decided to agree with her after all it was her personal life and in that situation I was a rank outsider.

But this certainly enraged me a lot. Why in any society it is little difficult to come in term with a fairer sex's success? And at the same time why always the relationship takes the first burnt of mistrust and face the trial of faith.

It was exactly after two days she approached me and wanted to talk to me. Situations like this bring out the little psychological counsellor in you and I decided to do that and give her a patient hearing and if possible dish out some sort of solutions. Frankly, for me handling the mundane of branch management was much easier than what I had in my hand. Still I took up the challenge and listened her out and with my little wit of everyday psychology I could find it was purely a miscommunication and little mistrust arising out of that from Rishabh's side. So, I suggested her some possibly probable solutions and she found some convincing to use. And it was a learning experience for me as I learnt keep things simple and honest and it would definitely work.

Rishabh was not ready to accept my solutions conveyed to him through her and he remained adamant about the whole issue. And what was scaring me when I found she was showing signs of slipping into depression. She was showing exhaustion and fatigue. Her frequent irritation and being abusive with her colleagues had put everybody in a surprise as these were contrary to her personality. So, one day I thought it had to end and decided to talk to her, as her behaviour was becoming intolerable for others. After initial hesitation she broke down like a little child in front of me and finally confided that Rishabh was not ready to yield an inch to her and was insisting on breaking the three year old relation, which to my understanding was always shaky and on a weak footing. It was late in the evening and outside chill had further chilled the room inside despite the room heater as I kept on listening her. And all the while I was thinking that what if the girl does something stupid. Whether I will be able to excuse myself for the whole chaos?

It was my suggestion that she should let the situation to take its own course without doing much of course correction exercises. This proved beneficial to all as she started showing signs of her old self. However, fate had some other plans for her. It was one message of Rishabh spelled and immediate for whom. Rishabh, as far as I understood, was off loading all her frustration on her. It was his failure to find a decent job coupled with her quick rise in the organisation was becoming unbearable for her. That day, one message from him was the final nail in the coffin. It was the end of relation from his side. And that evening she cried so much that paled the mighty Uttarakhand rain outside. I took some time to intervene and finally when I did she finally bared all her problems. It was quite natural on my part, who was trying to be a little more humane. That day for the first time I started disliking this boy Rishabh. My feeling was "she does not deserve her". That evening, for the first time after her arrival in my life, she showed some signs of being resolute, when she said, "no more I am going to accept his tantrums and it is over for once and all".

And that day I jumped in without really realising the final outcome would be a book.

Increasing friendship

Purple Lady is now showing signs of reviving herself after a big heart break. But the lurking phantoms of her past were scaring her and making her life miserable. Fortunately at times she was showing enough courage to fight those demons haunting her from her past. And like a Good Samaritan Kanisk was always there on her side to let her steer clear of the messy patch. But to my discomfiture unexpected twist and turns were affecting both of us. She is a big dreamer and mostly lives in a dreamy land of her own despite the ups and downs coming her way.

Now it was time to reason with her. Time to show her things in right perspectives so that she could distinguish and understand what was really right for her and also wrong for her. Her perception about her surrounding gradually changed as she started to comprehend that her opinion about things was not always true and what the environment was demanding was not always wrong. She started appreciating the rationale behind certain complex situations and stopped being sceptic and critical about everything. Situations for her and around her for others became very peaceful and cheerful, as it was her nature to make others happy and see them laughing. She started cracking jokes and playing pranks with her colleagues. This pleased all, including her parents and above all me also.

It was around groggily I answered her phone call that day. She was very excited as she had managed to get her mother's ascent to go to a movie with me. In fact it was I who had suggested her to get the permission from her superiors when she threw a movie offer with her on an office holiday.

And surprise of surprises she woke me up at around 6 in the morning and wanted to know whether I was ready. "Have you gone crazy", I found myself saying to her at a slightly agitated voice, "look at your watch it is just", before that she snatched away the conversation and said, "I am all ready for the film." I tried to search for excuses to steal some hours of sleep before going for the movie so enquired what about breakfast and she said in a jiffy, "a full glass of milk and two paranthas with some overnight left over vegetable curry."

It was around 8 AM when I looked at my mobile there were 15 missed calls and when I called back I had to face her full blast of anger. She was really angry with me with perhaps the whole world. "I hardly can wait for anything or anybody and for the first time in my life I waited for you." It took some time for the normalcy to return and finally let go the movie we had in mind and went for another. My feeling, that day, was movie was just an excuse for us as we saw less, smiled more and gabbed a lot and in between time flew like few seconds. For the first time I felt I should have tied time somewhere at least for the day for us only.

That night we talked and talked. It was like probing each other. While my sense said she was searching a person in me capable of taking care of her and I was trying to find out what was still bothering her.

Next day morning her red nose alerted me that I had missed some part of our conversation last night. In fact she kept on saying and kept on coming out and going back into sleep. So when she enquired about something I was totally blank and her nose turned red, signalling her temper. She was so angry she started crying and ....

I panicked for a while and then laughed at her state of condition. But, she did not give me a chance to pacify her. Finding no way out I gave her a big bear hug, it was much before the *Jadu ka Jhapi* medication. Suddenly everything changed in her. Those exquisitely carved eyes suddenly remained focused on my eyes, there was no surprise, in fact no emotion, only blank but intent stares, penetrating my inner self. Tears were drying gradually, we kept on staring at each other but the hug had not eased. The eyes were trying to tell many things, but the quietness in it, were spreading more than million untold but sweet words. I was just........... And she was also.............

And then the coming days were some of the best times we experienced in togetherness and came closer to each other. Suddenly the trust level had touched a new high; my ideas were like beacon of hope; her decisions were becoming valuable for me; in unison we were giving a new definition to our relationship. Everything was moving very fast.

They Climbed the Mountains

That day Kanisk was washing his dirty clothes. Not because, he was lazy but did not get time. The phone rang but I did not respond as I was determined to clean the mess then do anything. Finally when I finished and looked at my phone found there were 12 miss calls and all from her. Gathering all my courage I rang her up. There was no response. I was scared as I was not mentally ready for her verbal barrage. So, I started muttering my school prayer.

Instead what I was listening completely threw me off the hook. In a very soft and sedate tone she said, "My dearest mad man what you are muttering."

"Prayer!" I exclaimed at once.

"I am feeling bore", she said.

"Enjoy your Sunday with your family."

"There is none today. I am alone; they have gone far for a family function."

But, why telling me I asked myself. Was she telling me "join me at home." Ideas for a while ran thick and fast.

I found asking what was she expecting from me and she suggested "let us go out."

"But I will bring in friend", I said to which she objected.

"I cannot be free with you in their presence and comfortable also as I do not know them."

"That will not be an issue."

"Yes! That is the issue'"

Finally that day I made her understand my view point to which she relented and agreed lastly.

The destination was fixed, "Mussorie", the queen of hills. I borrowed a bike form my friend and took her on it. She sat in a typical Indian fashion, with both the legs on one side, which was left. At first she seemed to be enjoying the ride. However, as the roads became little different form plains she started to panic. Gradually she started to came little closer and hold me very tight. It did not take me long to realise why she was holding me in a tight grip. In fact she was afraid of the hilly road with sudden curves and speeding vehicles coming from opposite direction. Finally when I stopped she jumped out of the bike and meanwhile for a moment I lost myself in the beauty of Mother Nature in abundance around us.

"Hey! You poet do you have a plan to go or stay here for always", she said.

I turned back and asked her why she forced me to stop the bike, to which she said, "I was really scared looking at the road and the way you were driving."

"You sit like a boy with both the legs on either side, that will make you comfortable and also you will not get scared", I said to her.

She looked at my face which had a very unrecognisable expression.

"Ok!, do not you worry, I will not press the breaks hard and sudden to take advantage of the situation", I said as matter of fact. However, I was little scared how she would react to it.

However, to my surprise she did not say anything and said, "let us go", and then after a while with a mischievous smile she said, "but do not press the brake hard of or all of a sudden."

I was feeling little unsecured this time. There was a faint wicked smile on her face with thousands meaning into it. But, one thing for sure, when I became little secured within a few minutes, I found trust in her face in me. As she is slightly short in height I offered her a helping hand to sit in that position where she would have to keep her legs on either side. She took my hand and I kick started the bike and then we started tearing the wind.

Finally we reached Mussorie and had a grand time. The trip was one of the most memorable for all of us. However, as per the earlier decision we stated pushed up early so that we could reach in time. I dropped her a little distance away from her home and came back.

That night she broke all the small barriers between us as she bared her mind and said she was in love with me and look forward to settle down with me. However, for me, who is very much attached to his family and its values and tradition like majority Indians, I restrained myself and never gave her a chance to go much ahead.

Turning Phase of Light

There was a definite change in her and it was towards better. This was visible in her and all those associated with her, both personally and professionally, were noticing that. I was happy that at last she was in harmony with life and things were settling down for her in all fronts.

But, time always does not remain the same, as it changes its colour so fast and so soon, that it does not take long to turn topsy-turvy. That day she was really upset with herself and it would not have taken a professional to read it from her body language. She was restless and agitated. That morning she reported late in office.

She had been to the doctor as she had severe stomach pain. The diagnosis revealed that she had ovarian cyst, which becomes painful in some cases. The doctor advised her to undergo medication for a long time and to remain under some sorts of control. And when finally I confronted her she simply cried holding my hands for a long time. I tried to bring the situation under control and after a while she started to behave normal. Then only she bared her problem before me and asked, "why? It is always happening with me only." I had no answer to her question and I preferred to keep quite. Other than a few consoling words there was nothing I could spare for her at that moment and I was so upset with my helplessness.

However, despite my consoling words tears again stated rolling down her cheeks. I made her to look at me and suddenly she hugged me tight. The hug was so tight that for a while I felt little breathless. It was as if she was trying to search something in me and was not getting and was trying to squeeze it out with a tight hug. I was feeling little uncomfortable as there were quizzical eyes peering at us. There were many thoughts running in their mind and I was thinking whether they were holding me responsible for her behaviour.

She continued to probe me for answers about her problem ridden life and the way out of it and I was standing like a stone without really having any suggestion. Finally after a while I suggested her that she could try Ayurveda or Homeopathy. With this her mood changed and she agreed to the two suggestions. Then I asked her to proceed to her console and start to work as the peering had not stopped from the other side of my glass cabin.

That evening I dropped her back at her home with the bike borrowed from my friend. Very nonchalantly she suggested, when I was driving her back home, why I was not purchasing a bike and was depending on borrowing at time of need. My answer was "do not have money and do not want to borrow it from my father."

Next morning my call went unanswered and again she came late that day. I did not say anything knowing her medical urgency. However, I found her very relaxed and got into the job as soon as she arrived. I was also little relaxed seeing her being normal. During lunch she came to and informed that she had a discussion with a good homeopath at Chandigarh and the person had assured that it would be alright. But, he had advised her to be extremely cautious while under medication. I really felt relaxed.

Days moved ahead peacefully as her medication started.

Change of Scene

A month passed and the doctor suggested for medical verifications like x-ray and some other tests. Everybody was anxious about what would be the outcome of the tests done. Meanwhile, she thoroughly scanned the internet regarding her problem. And one such finding really distressed her. She found out that surgical intervention was possible to remove the cyst; however, she stood the chance of losing the chance of becoming a mother. And this she confided to me. This was the moment probably I was waiting for to stand by her side, in whom she had found a close confidante.

My offer to her was, I would marry her in case of such an eventuality. That day I told her, "hardly matters whether become parents or not because you matter most and nothing else to me." And in a long time I felt relieved that for the first time I was standing on her side like a real friend.

Meanwhile, I found her very happy. But, some facts kept hunting me. She belonged to an extremely rich and conservative Sikh family. And I am from Bihar. The impression her family carried about Bihari's was that we were either criminals or labours and nothing else. However, they forget that numerous bureaucrats Bihar has produced.

And on the other hand there were other problems at my family's end. I am a Brahmin from the Maithili society of Bihar. My society prefers that a boy must marry a Maithili girl and vice-versa, else this regarded as a blot on the family.

Purple Lady was aware all the hurdles of the conservative societies we belonged to and she was not very enthusiastic about the offer I had made. Then I came with another proposal.

"You can go ahead with anyone of your community once you get rid of this problem, I mean medication helps you", I said to her. There was no problem with me I assured her.

In the meantime, her problems were far from over. Sometimes the results were positive and sometimes they were not very encouraging. She continued to be tensed and it was natural on her part.

An unexpected encounter with a stranger

Made me fall in love

She was charming, beautiful, sensual and intelligent

Enough

To hold me high

And so did I

Stranger cared for me, loved me and liked me

Just like someone next after the lady who gave birth to me

She managed to hold my arms at times when I was depressed

Tried to rejoice me by the words that came out of her lips

Without fearing the world and without caring of what those words meant

Making me laugh and smile at every point of time

She turned up to be my life

The summer days, long

Shorter than previous day of my life,

Night at 2 seemed darker and longer

Beep my phone, I woke up

A text message wished me a beautiful time ahead in life

Truly, those messages always made my day bright

Slowly and sharply I loved her to a level

That it turned hard for me to think myself without her

The things were right, the things were wrong

The time went on, on and on...

We were happy

We shined like the sun

We made plans and carried on those

Fearing no one on this earth

We gazed the stars shinning at the dawn

We searched for the God in the half-phased sun

We searched for a life even in the melted ice

The time went on, on and on...

And

A moment came, when we parted of

It was not a joke neither was a fun

She took my heart and dropped me off

Left me alone to roam on the streets

And to gaze the skies with a tearful eyes

She didn't cheated me, nor did I

Actually the matter of fact, was that she is no more alive, for me

The God we searched in the half phased Sun

Took her away one night

I cried like a mad, I shouted like a crack

Now I am alone, on the busy streets

Was searching for her on the crowded roads

I loved her hard and I loved her soft

Now I miss her, in this golden heart

I really miss her and cry for her

I just pray to God, to keep me going

To break the ice of the dreams we saw

I am alone but yah happy a lot

I met a stranger who taught me love!!!

The Next Phase of Problems along with the Cyst

The days were going good with no question that haunted her into the emotional setback that always remained in her mind and heart. The only belief for the Purple Lady at this point of time was, seeing Kanisk standing on her side as a support system. These were the ugliest phase of ground realities that she was facing.

The worries went low not completely but of course to a level.

This helped her to think forward to the things and enjoy life. The months were passing and same was the situation of medications, which remained changing with the time with little modifications in the size of the cyst.

Meanwhile, all these circumstances of tragedies and traumas, she got engaged into the repulsive effect of the plans of her maternal uncle and grandfather.

As informed earlier in the very first chapter that she was a member of the family, where Kanisk did the campus recruitments at Dehradun and met her for the first time in life.

Her father, who was neither an employee nor a partner of the college, once took a serious decision of selling all his properties, gold and other belongings in Punjab. He sold each and every thing to support the cause of business of his wife's father and brother.

Till date, Kanisk remained in darkness in context of her family, or you can say he simply never understood the scene although demonstrated by the lady several times.

Actually, the ongoing scene at this point of time was that the institute lacked finances to start up a new course and take an affiliation to the same.

Purple Lady's uncle required a huge amount to provide the University Authorities visiting the campus to justify the affiliation and start the course.

Off course, the huge amount can be termed as happiness sharing tool under which the process takes place under the table. In India this action is termed as winning shot.

To make this shot her family, that is, they were forced to take a bank loan of about 20 lakh rupees. The loan takers included her father, mother, sister, and the 16 year old brother along with her.

The excellent part was that the maternal side of the girl asked them to not worry about the segment of loan, as it will be deposited with time.

But the scene changed soon with the departure of the University authorities. This was noticed after her family members started receiving calls from the bank requesting them to deposit the monthly instalments.

This news acted as the threat to Purple Lady's family. Her father, Kanisk's would be father-in-law, a mid height Sardar with big belly, took all the tensions on his head. Remaining quite he was searching forward to the aspects that would have helped his family from the challenges that beckon him and the family.

He was aware of the challenges lying ahead and the damages that his family could suffer if everything doesn't go well. Thus at times, he forced his brother-in-law to deposit the premiums and at times paid them himself.

The prevailing conditions and the financial environment of family were visible on the Purple Lady's face.

Kanisk had a role to play at this crucial time. His role was to make sure that the prevailing situations do not force Purple Lady to take a wrong step. He was worried about her health to, which could have suffered due to the distressed mind and heart.

He knew that the tough challenges ahead on her part, would affect him and his personal life. But being a man of word, he managed to stand by her side.

He always knew the promise that was made when he accepted her offer of being her life. He promised to not leave her even at dark times.

You can term, Kanisk was acting as a 'Tower of Unity' for her by standing on her side even after knowing the situations. This action of Kanisk helped him to win another pie of trust of his love, his life.

Her face was elaborating the happiness which was hidden within her heart. He was happy for choosing a guy as her life partner who was ready to face all challenges that were thrown on her way by the life.

Meanwhile, a day came, when duo entered into a question-answer hour, that they had several times before but never the sessions always passed just like nothing. But this time, they were serious and thus started throwing questions on each other. The questions and answers were a search that was the love is true or fake or something else, like an act of humanism that was being performed to make sure that the girl lives long.

The first a series of questions were thrown to Kanisk by the Purple Lady, later Kanisk did the same that she did.

Purple Lady: *Do you really love me or just trying to do favour on me after seeing me in a bad situation. (The question was thrown as Kanisk earlier never accepted her proposal to be her love but all of a sudden came forward to be a messiah for her at least in the condition she was going from).*
She further said, what makes you catch my hand at the moment when I am nothing. I am a girl who doesn't know what my future have in its stock for me.

Kanisk: *If you had not been my love then what was the thing that kept me stand by you even at the time, when I am able to see that nothing is going good in your life.*
Tears followed and he gazed her face like a child. Her eyes were saying that she was talking to a person whom she trusts and believe that he will never leave her alone.

Purple Lady: *Actually, as a matter of fact there exist numerous chances of my not being able to conceive, how come you* *agree to take the challenge? Don't you want to have a child of your own?*

Kanisk: *What remains if I am a father of my own child or a child that I adopt? If you can't conceive than it doesn't mean that you are not a women or there is any mythological penalty that threatens me from falling in love with you. Situations may prevail in my life, when you will be fine to conceive but may God take away my abilities of producing a child, so that problem hardly matters me.*

Purple Lady: *What about the big loans on my part taken by the maternal uncles on my name as well as the family?*

Kanisk: *It hardly bothers me, as if I have accepted you into my life than it mean that I have signed a treaty to deal with the problems that follows you. No matter how big it will be and how difficult it is, I will stand by your side always. Apart from that we are grown enough to help ourselves together against the loans.*

Purple Lady: *But why don't you allow me to inform any one of my family members or friends about your presence in my life?*

Kanisk: *Because I feel people will think that you were forced to think my way or my position made you fall for me. On the other hand, they may think that your richness is a cause that made me fall for you.*
Secondly, the thing will be like this till I am not able to convince my parents in regard to you and till then I don't

want the world to know about the things because it may hamper your reputation in public.

Many questions similar to this kept on floating and Kanisk kept answering. She ended with questions and now it was Kanisk's turn to thrown questions. He started throwing the same two questions.

Purple Lady: *when will you talk with your parents in regard to me?*

Kanisk: *The day my sister is married. Her marriage would give me the confidence that is required by anyone to inform their parents about his/her love. This confidence is a must at least in case of Indian middle-class family.*

Kanisk: *What is the reason that made you feel about me and accept me as a love of your life?*
The question was forwarded as she was the person who started the process of love and it took him about three months to say yes.

Purple Lady: *I don't know was the answer like always and turned the question with a statement that she was nothing without me and can't think of her without me. She replied the same that she loved me even more than her family and even more than God.*
This answer ignited confidence in Kanisk that he had made a right choice and was sure that he will be able to convince his parents for her at some point of time. He thought that way because he had his faith in a statement that studies:-

Do not wait; the time will never be 'just right'. Start where you are, work with whatever is at your command, and better tools will be found as you go along.

Kanisk: *Will you change for me even if I turn hard or harsh for you for sometime because of situations which may follow ahead in life?*

Purple Lady: *Are you mad that I will change and how can you think that way? This always remained an answer in a form of a question to me.*

After the question-answer session ended, Kanisk informed her that it will be difficult for him to convince his parents but requested her to not count him out of her life till I don't say complete no from their side.

But he also promised that he will revolt against their decision if your health problem remains to be in effect.

The evening ended with the row of questions and answers with a hope that everything will be fine.

Kanisk dropped her back to her home this evening. This time he used his own bike, which was purchased with an idea to drop her back every evening.

While returning back to his place, he received a call from the Purple Lady. She was crying. She was speechless.

He asked the reason for the tears which were visible in her eyes. She was not able to say a single word. After being forced, she informed that her father, who was on a counselling visit to Jaipur, met a heart attack.

Shocked Kanisk asked, is he alone over there or someone is there who can take him to a hospital.

30

She informed that her elder sister's colleague at Jaipur branch was available to help him out at such a challenging time. He admitted him in a hospital and paid the charges which were required to start the operation.

It was a good luck episode, as someone came forward to help him in a city of unknowns.

He took the challenge, admitted him and paid the huge charges of operations, which was put forward by the hospital management.

By now, he was well and got discharged after which her family managed to get him back to the Himalayan city, Doon. Doctors discharged him with a suggestion of not indulge in works that gifts tension to him, as it would manage to call him back to the condition from where he was being discharged.

The time crossed somehow leaving a pleasant note as his would be father-in-law was recovering at a great pace.

The Life on a Normal Routine with the Medications On

By now, Kanisk's **would be father-in-law was showing the positive signs of recovery as he started certain activities like climbing ladders**, going to the office and many more.

The most interesting fact for the management of college and tensed Kanisk was that the old man who met a heart attack few weeks back took back all those responsibilities, which were pending because of his absence from the work-ground.

Management was happy as it was the admission season and he was one of the best counsellors that the college had at that point of time.

Kanisk was tensed as he was aware that he is a person who loves doing his work without any worry of health.

Out of concern towards the Purple Lady and her family, Kanisk opted for a new habit and that was visiting a place to receive her in the morning for the office and drop her back to home, every evening.

She was a regular grocery and vegetable buyer of her home, almost every day. This habit of her forced Kanisk wait outside the store waiting for nothing.

On occasions the time of wait, which turned up to be more than 30 to 40 minutes made Kanisk feel pathetic. This wait for few minutes seemed as if he was waiting for some unknown since centuries.

As earlier said he never had a bad habit of waiting for someone, but in this condition the person who made him wait was his life.

His activities during this time of wait included moving out to some or the other street side food stand and have something, peep inside the store to make sure that she was fine, and many more.

One can easily term the activity of peeping into the store as extreme care or an extra pinch of possessiveness.

To be true, waiting outside of the store always made him feel as if he was just a driver to her who can't even go into the store to assist her purchase the materials required.

His anger at times, forced him into the store where he diagnosed that she had a bad habit of calling back to her parents, mainly Maa, to decide what should be bought and what not.

Under these conditions of picking, waiting outside a store and dropping, they also acquired a habit of skipping the lunch hours with the office mates. This bunking episode helped them to enjoy their meals together without any disturbance or you can say without being noticed.

Interesting factor the event was that Kanisk got an opportunity of having his first bite with the hand of person, whom he loved. In their love story, these moments can be counted as one of the loveliest moments for Kanisk.

The time went on, on and on, in the race of enjoyment and getting attached to each other to all the heights. They started dreaming of the days after which they will be engaged and then married to each other.

During this period of extra love and possessiveness, Kanisk managed to forget about her medications.

One day, he enquired the same and the condition of cyst which was troubling her.

Her reply was shocking as due to lack of finances she was not able to make a visit to the doctor, who asked her to be at his place with certain reports.

In anger, he took her to a clinic and forced her to get all the tests done including the x-ray and others. He collected the reports, got them scanned and also mailed them to the doctor, who was out of the city for some cause.

After reviewing the reports, the doctor replied back and the reply was a cause of celebration for both of them.

The report said that the size of the cyst was at the mode of collapse, or you can say it was at the last stage of treatment.

Closing his eyes, Kanisk thanked the God and then asked her to accompany him to a temple to thank him by offering prayers.

She agreed.

Next day, they visited a Temple. Kanisk thanked the God for hearing his prayers and helping her out of the pain that she was carrying in the abdomen and the heart.

Abdomen pain was due to cyst, while her heart pained, as she had a feel that the creator always chooses her for the punishment. He punishes her by one or the other way.

With time, Kanisk's attachment with her was getting much stronger.

Paranormal Activities and a new drama

It was time to rejoice at the home of the Purple Lady as one of her cousin, a resident of New Zealand, was supposed to visit her place.

Being a daring lady, one night she shared a story of film that she likes with the Purple Lady. The film was Paranormal Activity, which was available on YouTube. She also narrated few scenes of the film to the family members. Demonstration ignited Purple Lady to see the film, that to on a night after office hours.

After this, she started feeling that she is being followed by someone, whenever she is alone. Indirectly, the film was a proof of presence of ghosts that to in her bedroom.

The movie made her feel afraid of almost everything that was visible to her. She started calling Kanisk at nights to feel that she is secured but never cared that the guy on the other end is in a need of sound sleep.

Her new activity created a doubt in mind of Kanisk. Two thoughts were puzzling him, the first was that she is really afraid and the other said that Ghost was a new excuse to have talks from dusk to dawn.

Since Paranormal Activity, every night, he received a call from Purple Lady claiming that she was afraid and there was something that was troubling her. As per her, every night she heard some footsteps in the balcony and at times she saw a black cat on the nearby boundary walls of the house which was visible from the window of her room.

Her calls helped her in distracting from the thoughts that troubled her. **Every night, the two** talked till the dawn approached.

Neither any explanation nor any suggestion by him helped in dealing with the imaginative ghost was following her. As if he/she was free like anything and didn't had any other work other than following her.

May be possible, these night talks helped her in being out of tensions but it was affecting the health of Kanisk. These talks attracted sleepiness on his way.

Worried about the health issue that was approaching Kanisk, he practiced a therapy of short naps during work and whenever he was free from everything, including a call from the other side.

Rest part of sleep was completed on Saturday and Sundays, the official holidays, when she was busy at her home with her family.

Things continued to be same, almost every week as she kept managed to see the next series of the same movie.

This inherited fear via paranormal activity, forced her to call Kanisk without any thought. He never complained and she never understood the same.

But a day came, when he scolded her and also requested not to see such things that trouble her. This happened due to the frustration that was acquired due to lack of sleep at his end and the prevalent fear on her part.

Purple Lady: *What can be done with the thought that is prevalent in my mind and heart?*

Kanisk: *Nothing, just stop thinking about the subject.*

Purple Lady: *How?*

Kanisk: *How can I suggest the solution, it's your head that thinks that was thus you will have to find a solution for the same.*

Purple Lady: *If I knew the way than why I would have asked for a solution? If you have any solutions to my problem then gives it or just go to hell.*

Kanisk: *Mam, I think that I have a solution to the same but I believe that you will not consider it.*

Purple Lady: *What is it? Tell me.*

Kanisk: *Will you take it positively or not?*

Purple Lady: *Yes.*

Kanisk: *I think that a visit to a Gurudwara or a Temple may help you out of the situation. To be true it is a time to pray as only prayer is a solution to the fear. Even I chant few* *stanzas of Hanumaan Chalisa at times when I am afraid of something, it helps me every time.*

She agreed and asked him to be with her during the visit. He agreed.

Next day, she came to the decided place from where the duo was supposed to meet. Kanisk received the lady, troubled with imaginative ghosts, and rode towards the temple. They reached the temple around 8am, about two hours before the office hours.

The duo prayed the God. Kanisk prayed for her well being. He prayed for creation of a situation under which he will be able to ask her hand for lifetime from her parents after seeking blessings from his parents.

He was not aware about her prayer and the demand she put forward to the almighty.

Kanisk believed that he had demanded one of the toughest things from the God. He felt that his demand was a challenge for the almighty, as his prayer would force the God, before whom they prayed, to convince the Gods of two different religions to create a situation under which things moves on a positive line.

If heard, the prayers. Then it would have forced all Gods to call a serious meeting to discuss his situation which would have allowed Kanisk to have a talk with his parents, where they grant permission to him to go ahead.

Possibilities were there that during the meet, they may take a decision of punishing the guy for standing against the will of the democratic thoughts of his father.

The prayer was a challenge for the Gods to, as they were supposed to change the thought process of parents at both ends, which was difficult.

After completing prayer with tears that flowed internally inside the soul of Kanisk and forcing them to meet and decide his fate, they moved ahead to the office.

They were 20 minutes late to the office. After reaching the office, Kanisk handed over the Prasadam (Sacrament) to one of office boys and asked him to distribute it among the teammates.

Positive change of the visit to the Temple was quite visible on the face of Purple Lady as it seemed as if she was out of the fear that haunted her for past fifteen days or more.

The positive changes made them to share their happy moments on phone after the office hours. At times, they discussed things like the way she will have to behave when she visited the paternal place of Kanisk in Bihar after they are married.

They also quarrelled on a question that what will happen of the son/daughter who was either adopted or born if the complications of cyst ended for life time.

They debated what if the child is a boy then will he be a Sardar with a Turban and a Kripaan - the Holy Sword with all the other belongings that a person from Sikh Community carried or a typical Brahmin with half bald head and a pony flowing from the centre just like Chanakya with chandan on the forehead.

Things went on and off as discussions never ended with a right conclusion.

Finally they concluded on a point that if the child is a son then he will be the beginner of a new religion in this world, a person who will carry a turban along with a Janew (Sacred Ceremonial Thread) along with a Holy Sword.

He will be a genuine mixture of humanity and a mix and match of the two religions, who will preach best things to everyone. He will try to end the problems of cast and religion from the earth. His efforts will make earth a liveable place where days and nights will pass with smiles and laughs.

Situation of Office Mates

The days were moving at the same pace with discussions including when I will dare to inform his parents about the other. The answer always remained the same, the day when my sister gets married.

Duo also had discussions on the traditional values and customs of the two families. At times, the discussions ended in fights due the tradition on Kanisk's side in which ladies cover their head in front of elders as a symbol of respect.

Meanwhile, the colleagues came to a state-of-mind that something was being cooked, between the Purple Lady and Kanisk. They also asked them about the probability of love between the two.

But the response was always the same that we are just friends nothing else.

Few who were convinced by the response offered suggestions that to free of cost that you two should look forward.

The promise at either side stopped us to unveil the hidden secret to anyone.

But, the hidden love story was on the move, the reports of the cyst were turning up to be normal. The problems always existed at her part by now, and the best part of their love was that Kanisk was ready to accept her in all formats.

There were people like the Hary, Nath, Ishu and others, who always suggested Kanisk to re-think his decision.

They tried to convince both by different mode of comments like you make the best couple; you understand each other like anything and many more.

But the reality was yet unknown to them.

Hary Singh, the person who was regarded as an elder brother by Kannisk and off course a mentor at times, also poked him by taking him and the Purple Lady to a Gurudwara so that the two can share good time with each other.

He did it with a thought that these journeys may end up into a relationship.

But the truth was that our relationship was already blessed and protected from Wahe Guru, Sai Nath, Lord Shiva and Goddess Durga. But yes it's true, every time while entering the Gurudwara, I prayed please make sure that the things go right.

A Small Picnic with the Office mates

Our client informed that due to certain technical problems, they will not be able to provide work for the day. This means a day less work on our part or you can say a day of enjoyment.

Thus, they (the team) planned a picnic for everyone, somewhere in a national park at a distance of nearly 30km from the office.

Next day, the bikes and cars were ready to move on. The eating materials to be used for preparation of food were put in the car. Knowingly, teammates planned to make Purple Lady sit on my bike.

The bikes were racing with each other.

It seemed as if they planned to provide some space to the love birds so that they can carry on a romantic journey without interruptions.

I, Kanisk, a speed lover, was driving at a slow pace. I was driving slow with an aim to talk about the journey and explain the recipe of the dish that was supposed to be cooked at the place of visit.

Yes, I was the chef for the occasion because each one wanted to taste the famous dish from Bihar named Litti-Chokha. These two delicacies, behaves like husband and wife to each other.

On arrival to the venue, the carpets were laid down to make each and everyone sit to carry on with the activities.

This was the day, when the Purple Lady seemed perplexed.

Being the chef of the occasion, I had less time to ask the reason for the situation but tried to ask the same via eyes and the response was nothing.

I thought she was jealous of seeing other girls sitting around me and smiled to continue with the work.

I also knew that my movement from the place would have not allowed anyone to fill their tummies.

While the dish was being roasted, I made an excuse with friends and moved on towards her and shared few steps in form of short walk.

I tried to enquire the reason of being perplexed and was informed that her mother was asking her to be back soon. This was the first time, when she was lying.

Shocked and amazed but not willing to spoil the mood of celebration, I went back to serve them as a chef again.

By this time, the lunch was over, they enjoyed the trip for an hour or two more and moved back to their homes.

While being back from the spot of picnic, I tried to discover the truth behind the hurry and the worried attitude of her. But no reply was returned.

The day ended and the night came, I called her back to beg an apology if something wrong happened. But the reply was can you please leave me alone for some moment.'

The Trauma that She Gifted

Amid the discussions and the allotment process, Kanisk's phone rang. She was the Purple Lady. On receiving the phone, she informed that she was with a new boy named Sachin, a person who was turning up to be closer to her.

Yes, he knew that the guy is a friend of some of her friends who have a habit of making deals and sign contracts of getting two people engaged and making them fall in love. One among them is a person who proclaimed that her sixth sense allowed her to feel what was right and what was wrong for the Purple Lady. Via these dramas, she always managed to win her confidence.

She informed Kanisk about the guy when she moved on to meet him for the first time. But on this day, it was informed that since then she has been meeting him on different occasions. Some of those meets were known, while many were not.

On her arrival, she seemed to be little puzzled and depressed. Initially, Kanisk thought not to interfere in her personal matter, thus remained silent.

But the mad love didn't allowed him to be a silent monk. He interfered with a hope that she will inform something about the happening of the day, may be that she is dating the guy.

But the answer landed on a different track. She said that the guy was forcing her to fall in love with him. Mistakenly, the guy thought that few meets were my love for him.

Kanisk smiled and said than what's the problem move on with him. He said so, because at this point of time, Kanisk was clear that she always thought of her own satisfaction and hardly cared of the one who loved her, whether the new guy or he himself.

She said that the circumstances of her life and the friends, who accompanied her during Kanisk's absence from the office made her fell a prey to him. But, now the boy has turned abusive and his over possessiveness was troubling her. She feared him.

Kanisk anyhow managed to console her. He wanted to ask her that was she dating the boy keeping him in the extreme end of the darkness about her life in his absence. But the question remained hidden in one corner of the heart - as Kanisk really cared and loved her - even after knowing things that was going on. Kanisk knew that if he leaves her at such a point of time than she would have been lost in the world of unfair circumstances.

He enquired, do you rely on me? Or can you trust me once again? Holding back the tears, which was about to flow from his eyes for two reasons, few for being cheated and the second was for her condition. This was the day, when she promised him not to hide anything and he promised once again of being hitched up with her under every circumstance, but would have been able to talk with his parents after sister's marriage was over.

Then, Kanisk managed to take her back to work as he believed in the fact that once you make yourself busy, you manage to forget the thoughts that troubles you, in the lonely hours.

That evening once again, he carried her back to her home on my bike. It seemed that she was not able to witness the tears in Kanisk's eyes, which flew continuously with the wind on the roads. He cried on the roads because of the feeling that he was unable to share his point with her. He had no words, but controlling every thought he definitely declared himself to be a guard for her in this unknown city of odds.

Now, Kanisk's daily duty was to travel a distance of 17 kilometres every morning to take her to the office. He picked her up from a pre-decided destination, so that her parents may not make him fell a prey to their anger. Every evening, he had the duty of dropping her back to her home. All this was being done to re-install the feel of safety and make her feel that his confidence on her was not lost.

During these days of being a driver from a lover to her, Kanisk managed to ask her that can we get married earlier, as soon as my sister gets married whose marriage was scheduled by the year end. She informed that her sunshine carried information that if she gets married to someone before attaining the age of 25, the marriage would end-up into a divorce or the life will remain trouble ridden. Hence, Kanisk agreed to the viable point in which she and her family believed in and was ready to wait for the time when she attains 25 and by that time he would have been of 28.

The Changing Tone of the office and the effects of Euro Zone Crisis

The Euro Zone crisis was looming large on Kanisk's mind as it was affecting the overall office scenario. The immortal shloka of Gita, about Karma, *Karmanye Vadhikaraste, Ma phaleshou kada chana, Ma Karma Phala Hetur Bhurmatey Sangostva Akarmani*, was the sole provider of solace to him.

Amidst all these one fine morning the MD called and asked Kanisk to fire 20 employees, with immediate effect, as budgetary constraints were looming large to take hard decisions. This was like a bombshell to him, because, they were all part of his team, which he had made with painstaking effort, bricks by bricks. And this was a big issue at hand and his turbulent love story took the back seat.

Then started the session of brain storming, with trusted aide Harry Singh. Step by step all the financial angles were looked with all seriousness. All types of permutations and combinations were carried out. Finally it was decided that the salaries of the employees would be reduced by 15% percent and five persons would be sacked. Those persons would be sacked who were working for earning that extra pocket money.

The best thing that emerged that those being sacked agreed to the proposal given the situation. The next best thing was maximum jobs could be saved. Kanisk gave a call to the MD and apprised him about the whole arrangement. He agreed after some logical points were put before him. The Euro Zone-Crisis took its first toll.

The Days after the Salary Slash

However, it was not easy on the part of the employees to digest salary slash, and this reflected in the whole atmosphere at the work place. Questions came thick and fast to Kanisk. He was the receiving end. Some took him seriously and understood the situation and some were sceptical about the whole scenario. Purple Lady was amongst those who were sceptical about the future of the company and its attitude towards the workforce.

Exasperated and frustrated with the questioning and scepticism Kanisk decided to speak to the MD and ask about bringing in some new projects so that it would boost the morale of the employees. He was told to have patience while, the company had taken his advice seriously. Meanwhile, his own suggestion that he would explore for more work on his own was also given a nod.

One evening Kanisk received an urgent call from the head office to come to Delhi. The news was discussion was on with a new client. He rushed through the evening and caught the last bus to Delhi and reached early morning, unaware of that something was waiting for him with the strength to change both his professional and personal life.

It was around 12.30 the MD asked him to accompany him. They discussed extensively about the company and its future and he also wanted to know about his personal and professional future plans. And this was for the second time he was asking him the question.

They entered the Barista, Noida. Kanisk was thinking the MD's client was coming there, however, contrary to his anticipation the MD wanted to know more about the Dehradun operation.

He was surprised when the enquiry became little ugly as it became personal and Kanisk asked him to explain the whole thing in details. When the real situation unravelled he became aware that he was caught in the web of office politics and had lost his credibility. He did not want to know who played the dirty trick.

Instantly he took the decision to offer his resignation and informed this to his MD. His only concern was that the salary of his employees should be brought back to normal position. He was no more interested about the politics and who did this, as his own self-respect was at stake. Even this would take him away from his lady love still self-respect was more important to him.

Next day Kanisk was back at Dehradun and kept himself busy with his official work. Neither he interacted nor involved himself in anything considered frivolous. Even he did not speak much to Purple Lady. Meanwhile, he learnt an audit team from Delhi had reached Doon to probe into the affairs of the branch including his. Came evening, as per his daily routine, he accompanied her back home, and on the way told her everything. However, that evening, her approach to him and his problem, gave him immense inner strength to fight any odd stood up to any eventuality.

Her words reassured him that there was no force which could harm him. However, he was in no mood to continue with the company. He was wondering whether he was continuing simply for the salary parity of the team, as promised by the MD or for Purple Lady.

Meanwhile, Kanisk applied for the government job of Indian Information Service. Few months passed finally the salary of the staff was restored back and true to his words Kanisk mailed his resignation letter to MD. The very next day, which was a Sunday, the MD was in Doon branch. He wanted an urgent meeting of the staff. The meeting was just farce. Finally the MD tried to convince him to not to leave the organisation. Even his team mates pressurised him. He remained stuck to his own principle. On the other hand he was wondering about the real intention of the MD. Somehow he got the feeling that the MD was trying to give a different picture before the whole team, that he was not in favour of Kanisk leaving the organisation, and was trying to gain a kind of image.

Finally the D day, or the day to quit arrived. It was 7th of June, 2012, a Thursday. He was supposed to handover the charges to someone, a nominee of the MD. By now, his responsibilities were being shared by three, including his lady love. There was a restiveness amongst the staff, it was probably for the change that was going to come. And Purple Lady was behaving little different at the least and erratic at the most. She was silent and seemed to be lost somewhere and was responding very absent minded if anyone asks her anything. Sometimes she was looking at Kanisk who was about to leave. Kanisk tried to find out her state of mind but she asked not to be disturbed and left alone.

But, how can she be left alone. Kanisk continued to probe her to make her normal. She was in no mood and continued to behave indifferently. He was trying to relieve her of her pain or agony but there was hardly any response from her. And this was perhaps for the first time he failed to convince her or to get any reciprocation from her. Kanisk tried to annoy her so that she would explode but, nothing happened. It was as if she had gone into a kind loneliness where she wanted no interference. For the last time he had an official lunch with the whole team. He forced her to join the rest in the last official lunch, which she finally did with smile on lips but tears ready to roll down from her eyes. To cheer her he informed her that he would be in the city for few months and would come every day to meet her.

Being the last day in the office, Kanisk had lots of impossible tasks to accomplish like convincing the team not to arrange any farewell party as it was not easy for him to part away from a company which was nurtured like his own child, leaving back Purple Lady and many more.

Finally one of the girls, Herlina, suggested for an outside party, which Kanisk agreed, and it was to be on the weekend. Gradually the entire office left as the official hour came to an end. It was Purple Lady and Kanisk, the two were left alone in office. He wanted to know, why she was around so late. To which she answered, "ever since we have come closer, never ever I have been to home without you dropping me back. It was for this reason, you bought the bike and today you ask this question."

He did not say anything. After a while he informed her that he made a false promise to the team that he would be around for the weekend party.

Retirement and her emotional crackdown

Finally the day of retirement or day to end association with the company came. It was 7 June 2012 (Thursday). Kanisk was supposed to hand over his charge to anyone of his teammates or anyone suggested by the MD.

By now, Kanisk's works were shared among three including his lady luck, the Purple Lady.

This was the day when few were trying to hold the ruckus created due to administrative changes, while the idiot Purple Lady was lost in something. She was silent and lost somewhere and was just gazing her love, who was about to leave the place, on a permanent basis.

In a trail, Kanisk tried to break her silence and bring her back to the place by questioning, where she is? What's going on in her mind? He asked the reason for being perplexed.

The answer was, nothing and please don't disturb me.

Why shouldn't I!!! Mam.

She wanted to be alone at this point of time. But the poor love, didn't allowed Kanisk to be silent. Curious lover!!! pitched in and asked the reason for the loneliness, which was visible on the face.

He tried to provide best solution to the problem she was going through but all went in vain. This was the first time, when the lover was not able to make her understand nor was able to understand her.

He was trying with a hope that the things in mind will be vomited soon and continued throwing Yorkers and Firkis'.

It was the time for lunch and like every day they both skipped the lunch to make sure that they can have an official lunch for the last time. After everyone was over with the lunch, Kanisk asked her to accompany him for the lunch but she was in no mood.

But, he forced her to join him on the last lunch in office. She joined him with a smile with tears in her eyes, which was clearly visible.

To cheer her, he informed her that he will be in the city for few months and will be visiting her almost every day in morning and evening.

The lunch was over amid the talks and explanations.

Being the last day in the office, Kanisk had lots of impossible tasks to accomplish like convincing the team not to arrange any farewell party as it was not easy for him to part away from a company which was nurtured like his own child, leaving back Purple Lady and many more.

On several explanations, one, the tallest-girl from the team Herlina said lets have a outside party on the weekend.

Kanisk made a fake promise of being in the party and moved on the works, needed to be completed on the day.

Finally, he was able to free himself from the shackles of responsibilities with which he landed Dehradun on 5 November 2010.

The working hours ended and slowly the teammates went off. But the Purple Lady was available in the office.

On being asked the reason for stay, the reply was let me know a day when I left the office since we are together and as far as I remember, you bought the bike just to accompany me back to home, if I am not wrong.

Nodding the head, he said let me complete the work then and typed the final and you can say a goodbye mail to the management and teammates.

Meanwhile, Kanisk informed her that he made a fake promise to the team about his availability somewhere for a weekend party.

Soon, they left the office.

Days after Kanisk left the company

Life has to go on so it goes on. Kanisk started his preparation for the Indian Information Service and for that he joined a coaching centre for additional help in getting ready for the examination. Meanwhile, his life went on as usual other than not being in a job. It was time for studying and ferrying her to the office and brings her back at the end of the day and drop her at her home. Kanisk was enjoying this bit of thing in his otherwise bland life.

Meanwhile, the little saving he had managed from his previous job was draining. Meanwhile, he planned to go back to his home and meet his parents and sister, who was going to get married soon.

After his return to the city he changed his abode fists to a single room, to save money and his habit of eating out in street side eateries. But, this did not go unnoticed to Purple Lady. One day she wanted to know why Kanisk, whom she knew as a voracious eater and had the reputation for it, was restraining himself or was not indulging in it.

To this he threw a very cautious answer, he was trying to concentrate on studies and not distract himself.

Finally the time for Kanisk came to leave the city. Before leaving he asked her to wish him luck for the impending exam after his return from his home. He specifically wanted her to wish him on the day of his paper. It was impossible for him to imagine times ahead as the day for him always begun with her voice.

Kanisk left Dehradun and the Examination

It was 21 July 2012 and Kanisk was supposed to board the train– Dehradun-Delhi Satabadi Express at 5am. The train timings, didn't allow him to have a sound sleep.

On the way, he met one of his ex-colleagues who worked with him in the same company but left after six months of joining. She too was heading to Delhi to appear the same examination.

Mundane discussions, like her new company, preparations for the examination and even movies did not let us know when the distance of 250 kilometres passed. However, she was genuinely shocked when she listened Kanisk's past experience and the reason for him leaving the company. She was well aware, it was Kanisk who single handed set up the branch and gave a solid foothold to the company in Doon.

Colleague: What's next?

It was extreme hunger, which took them to Coffee Home, at Connaught Place, which was incidentally one of the most favourite hangouts for Kanisk.

He felt the silent tickling of the mobile in his pocket when he was putting the order. It was Purple Lady at the other end and she was enquiring about his journey. Kanisk informed him everything and what he was doing at that moment, and the last information was enough to draw sharp reaction from her, as she heard the name of Sweta. Either it was jealousy or sheer possessiveness, that she fired hundreds of questions. Finally she hung up the phone, whether she accepted the explanations remained a million dollar question for Kanisk. After lunch each left for own destination, but never forget to wish best of luck for the examination.

Soon Kanisk called his lady love again. She answered in a manner as if she had bitten thousands of red chillies. There was no change in mood and she kept on taunting him for his meeting with Sweta. She was in no mood to listen to any justification or any reasons. It was as it she had decided her mind about the whole episode. Realising the futility of making her understand Kanisk told her to hang up the phone so that he would call up his friend Sunny, who would come to receive him at the metro station. Sunny and Kanisk were friends since their under-graduation days at Rourkela Institute of Management Studies at Rourkela.

Sunny met him at the metro and took him to his one room apartment. Kanisk waited for the 'best of luck call' from Purple Lady, but it never came. He finished his examination and proceeded to his hometown as the next most important thing for him was his sister's impending marriage. From station he tried to contact her but there was no response from her and finally when she answered it was for very brief period. And when he asked him why he did not wish him the reply was, "busy with some work and further there was no balance in the phone."

Kansik reached his hometown and got busy with the preparation of his sister's marriage. He took a local number for the period and passed on it to his lady love. However, there were very less number of calls from her side except from the customary good morning and good night messages. Probably, the daily busy schedule was preventing her, thought Kanisk.

He had to book an early ticket back to Delhi as he got an offer from another company and they wanted a formal discussion at the earliest date possible. This was informed to Purple Lady. Meanwhile, the date for his sister's marriage was fixed, 9th December 2012. Kanisk had decided that he would speak to his parents after the marriage, so very carefully he was painting the picture of Purple Lady before his parents for their approval on a later date. However, his sister picked up some cue and kept on asking him about her and wanted to know if there was something serious between them, to which Kanisk would just laugh.

Kanisk was Back to Delhi and his Mission Job

Kanisk's search for job continued as he was already two months off it. So, he came back to Delhi and stayed with Sunny to appear for some written followed by interview, which were scheduled for the month of August. As there were time for him for the interview, Kanisk thought of going to Dehradun and meet his lady love. So, he boarded a bus to the capital city Uttarakhand and informed his roommate Maddy. He called up Purple Lady and informed her about his visit to Dehradun. They fixed up a rendezvous next day evening.

The meeting was fixed at four o' clock but before that he called her to make sure when she would be free of her work. Those were the days it was the stress of her job, as she was overloaded with work, was making her forgetful. So, Kanisk did not receive any phone call nor reply to his messages.

For a moment he was sceptic about her intention and different thoughts came to his mind. "Has she changed?" he kept on asking then smiled at own folly. He rang her to ascertain when she would arrive and the answer was in ten minutes. But, the ten minutes stretched to one hour and forty five minutes. And Kanisk kept himself waiting for her arrival and the sheer thought of meeting her hardly affected him.

However, when she arrived there was hardly any remorse or anything she started showering barrage of accusative questions. Those were harsh still Kanisk bore with and gave her a smile full of intentions, which could never be doubted. Rather he begged excuse to her. She was looking extremely alluring to him. Controlling his emotions he asked about her well-being which she replied in affirmative. She said, "you are responsible for I remaining well and energetic, and being more responsible."

Kanisk was happy with her professional progress. She was now handling a whole team now, who were very much new to the whole system of functioning and were finding it hard to grab the things. And above all had loads of attitude. Besides, he was aware about the demand of the client of the Doon branch as these bunch of unprofessional were demanding in nature and were always hell bent upon finding out some kind of errors in the work.

She asked Kanisk to drive fast as he was very slow. He knew why she was telling so. As old habit both of them go to the market where she would be purchasing daily essentials for her home and he would help her in this. Kanisk informed that he was in the city just for two days as he was supposed to face the interview two days later. She was happy listening to what he said, but the real reason one day she might go to Delhi.

Before departing Kanisk asked her to keep herself free by 3 PM so that they can meet again. In the course of things he rang her up again to know whether she remembers that they were meeting next day. Then he asked her a very silly question, whether she had reached safely at home, to which she answered, "have you gone mad or crazy, you dropped me at home." To this Kanisk replied, "I am the maddest or the craziest." Then at her request Kanisk recited a poem to her over phone the main theme was how much he had pain endured when she did not call him.

Next day morning he rang her up to remind her that she should make herself free by 3 PM as they were going to meet. However, she put a little if into it. She asked Kanisk to finish some of her editing jobs so that she would be free, to which he agreed, and a mail arrived soon. Kanisk finished the file work within two hours and mail her back. Within 15 minutes he reached the designated spot where they were supposed to meet. And she also reached the spot after ten minutes. They discussed about the plan for the day.

For some time they argued about where to visit, finally as Kanisk threw the ball in her court she suggested about going to a particular abode of Lord Shiva, the TapkeshwarMahadev. Kanisk had never been to there during his stay at Doon, so he asked her to be the navigator. However, one thing Kanisk found irritating, as soon as they reached there she said she would not enter the temple as she was having her period at that moment. Rather she asked him to go alone, to which Kanisk did not agree. He said that he would come when both would be able to enter the temple. Then they drove towards the Robbers Cave. Here they, away from human habitat and prying eyes, they hugged each other. They remained in that state for a long time and did not speak a single word. Then they drove aimlessly and came back to have their food at their favourite old joint. It was getting dark so Kanisk drove her back and dropped her at her home.

None wanted to depart, as the moments, the silence, the body language, everything was............ That night Maddy, his old roommate at Doon dropped him at the bus stand and he caught the night bus to Delhi and attended the interview next day. The interview went well and the interviewer informed that the results would be out in a week time. Soon Kanisk, after coming out of the interview room, informed his Lady Love that he was coming for two days to Doon, but failed to understand her reaction.

Back in Dehradun and changes

Kanisk was back in town and went to the same place where they used to meet. He waited for more than an hour as she took some more time to arrive. There was hardly any reaction on her face. Every question asked was evaded with some or other excuses.

In a day or two after his return the result for the IIS examination was out and Kanisk had made it. He was hoping she would jump in excitement or behave something like this but none happened when he broke the news to her. This further disappointed him. Meanwhile, his friend Nitish asked for his resume as there was a vacancy for which fitted Kanisk. He got the call for the interview a day after he sent his resume. This he informed to her lady love and again the reaction was not very encouraging and every time his heart sank a few notch.

Kanisk got the job and was asked to join immediately. He came back to Doon and informed her about the success and also he was leaving soon. And after a day he moved out of the town with his baggage. It was the month of September 2012 and he left the city and joined at New

Delhi. And she made an important declaration for all these she was restraining herself when they were meeting.

He phoned her and informed her about the job. In reciprocation she informed him about the constant grilling, in a typical Indian fashion, she was facing regarding him. Who was he? How their relation is? All sorts of concerned questions from family members.

Kanisk did not say anything but decided in his mind. Once he makes it through the interview of IIS he would ask her hand from her parents and would also speak to his parents in this regard. Meanwhile, radio became his friend and especially one programme "Yadon Ki Idiot Box with Nilesh Mishra' became his favourite. The short stories those being told by Mishra were really realities of life and were very close to him.

The day of interview came and Kanisk was preparing him for the D Day. There were five interviewers inside, whom he faced after the initial verification of the documents. The interview was tough and they tried nail him from all angles, which he to his level best tried to defend and tackle.

Introduction of a stranger and Purple Lady's visit to Delhi

A week passed by after Kanisk left Doon for Delhi. Within this one week, for God knows the only reason, they never spoke to each other. It was a Sunday, after five days, his phone rang. It was purple lady on the other side. As usual she started firing away her questions and like a tamed puppy, Kanisk kept on listening. The questions were ususal, why he was not calling; how he was keeping and so on.

It was during those staccato question session she suddenly wanted, it was rather a nice surprising disclosure, Kanisk to find a job for her at Delhi. She was finding it difficult to be at Doon without him. It was a big sweet shock and soon he asked for her resume.

And after two days Kanisk rang her up and wanted to know whether she had received any interview call or not. To which she replied in affirmative and informed her that she was coming with her mother on the next Saturday for that only.

And on Friday she was at Delhi with her mother and was staying hardly a kilometre away from his house. It was the house of her close relatives. Kanisk wanted to meet and the biggest challenge was her mother. Finally Kanisk managed to get the permission, for half an hour only, over phone from her mother. The time allowed was only for thirty minutes.

That day he rode like a race bike rider and jumped two traffic signals. In love and war everything is fair, said the greatest lover Lord Krishna, so two signals were just nothing. That was Navaratra time the roads were crowded.

He found her at the designated spot.

She was wearing a red hot top and slacks. The slacks were not certainly complementing her still she was looking, as usual, gorgeous. Without wasting time she jumped on to the bike and they sped away. The time was very short. Near the Community Centre where the Navaratra was being celebrated they stopped. The two weeks separation had made him like, cannot be described lover, and he kept on looking at her speechless. She suddenly said she was feeling uncomfortable with his gaze and distracted him. Finally she asked him to go the nearby bookstall and purchase some novels. Kanisk made the payments. Those were gifts for her. Meanwhile, the phone rang. It was her mother, who was reminding her that it was already thirty minutes, the allowed time for them to meet.

The two immediately rushed to her relative's house where she was staying and Kanisk dropped her there and she rushed without even saying a goodnight.

Next day Kanisk asked her about her plan, and she informed that she was meeting some of her friends. That was a Sunday and as usual, he visited the Coffee Home at the Connaught Place, his favourite joint. This is the place he would gel with his friends of college days. That day he was early and kept on waiting for her friends.

Meanwhile, he rang her up. There were lots of disturbances at the background when she picked up the phone. Kanisk wanted to know where she was, and she informed, she was at 'Hokkar Bar' at Connaught Place, with her friends. Soon he found himself asking, whether they could meet, which she avoided little awkwardly.

Suddenly he had the feeling that she was slipping away from him. The puppy intuition had smelled that. He could feel what was in offing for him. But the mind was not ready to accept the thought.

The Days of Retreat and Remembrance

He made a very painful decision that he would make less calls and would concentrate on his work more to surmount the pain that had befallen on him. At least the work was there for him to tackle the touchy situation through which he was passing.

Suddenly there was a perceptible change in him. He became a workaholic as he doubled his production. This was a challenge for his colleagues. There were faces all around as his performance would set a different benchmark for others. This was helping him, and dead tired he would come home, after putting in twelve hours and would go to sleep without any problem or unnecessary disturbances.

For his colleagues and bosses, this behaviour of Kanisk remained a mystery. They kept on wondering. Meanwhile, there was no communication from her at least there was no information regarding her interview. However, he was sure that she will pull through the interviews.

Finally she was called for the interview. Suddenly she started calling him. Again the old vibe was back between them. The tame puppy, which had got angry, was back again inside Kanisk. She was enquiring how she would face the interview; how she would bargain for her salary; and so on. Meanwhile, there was also the same old cajoling that she loved him most. He was the only one whom he cared. Kanisk was happy with all these blah, blah and blahs. Even at times the feeling came that the messages, which he was receiving form her, were actually meant for someone else. However, he cherished those messages and kept them without deleting like precious possessions.

Finally her day of interview. And they decided to meet after that part is over and discuss at least something about their future. Kanisk called his friend Sunny, who was facing another interview in the same company and asked him to accompany her. For the first time Sunny came to know about her. Sunny, after the interview, would drop her back at the metro from where Kanisk would pick her up.

Sunny, a true friend, always stood beside Kanisk. As per the plan he dropped her at the place where they were supposed to meet, at the metro station. They sat and had very few words, but there was nothing about the misconception, created in the interim period. Finally Kanisk dropped her back at her relative's house.

Next day she received a call from the company confirming her about her selection. Now it was her time to face the challenges to convince her family members to move to Delhi. She definitely had a tough time in her hands ahead. She was the person who would take care of all the major problems of the family. And leaving those behind and moving to Delhi for her was little difficult and also for all in the family.

And again she managed to pull Kanisk towards her once again. Kanisk always stood by her during all her problematic days and the family also.

She got busy planning about the impending prospect of moving to Delhi. She planned to have a new look in the new city. She wanted to cut her hair short, which he protested, as she was a Sikh girl and was against the religious decrees. Finally she convinced him. Finally she sent me the list of all the things she wanted to purchase on line and I approved those. She purchased those and Kanisk made those payments, and this he came to know when the message from the credit card service flashed on his computer and mobile screens. She proudly said she had used her card, to which Kanisk did not say anything. In reply Kanisk send her a smiley. Meanwhile, she mailed her resignation letter to the MD and HR of her previous company.

Kanisk, meanwhile, got busy with the preparation of her little sister's marriage. This was coming close. He was supposed to be back to home for few days for the ceremony. Meanwhile, his other big target was to make the disclosure to the family regarding the presence of Purple Lady in his life. He was happy now as they were going to meet soon and he was going to tell it to the family. These were blissful experiences for him and can never be explained in words.

Finally she arrived in the city on 25th November, 2012.

Her Arrival in the City, Delhi-NCR

Sunday, 25th November 2012, it was 5:30am when my phone rang with an exciting voice, now we have the chance of meeting every evening. Let start it from today itself, after all it's a weekend.

The impatient Kanisk had a sleepless night with a hope to meet the lady the next day. Drenched in the thoughts, he kept messaging with a pray for a safe and comfortable journey.

But at the same time, he was worried because her mom was accompanying her. This was going to be his first time when, he was going to face her face-to-face. He knew that the mom was going to stay with her for more than a day or two; this would have helped aunt to make sure that her daughter is safe in the new city to all the levels, before leaving.

Being scared of creating a negative aura on the very first meet, he managed to stop himself for the day and planned to meet her on Monday, the second day of hers in the city. It was a challenge for me to hold my anxiety to meet her; after all, he was waiting to get a simple hug from her.

The day ended, on phone calls and regular enforcement of law from her end and my pressure to meet on the same day. I lost the battle, not because it was hard to win over her, but the reason was I was always happy to see her win in every venture and every fight of the life, may be possible either it was with me.

During the calls, Kanisk was informed about the monetary problem that she landed due to over investment on day one in the city. The answer was, will try making sure that money reaches in time, so that she can manage to pay the advance money as rent to the PG owner

Today, Kanisk took a half-day off from the office to make sure that he catches her glimpse at the earliest. But the same traffic of Delhi delayed the plans.

The best part of the meet was that he never wanted to have such encounter with his future mother-in-law but it happened. The Purple Lady was standing near the metro station along with her mom.

However, Kanisk managed to move ahead and touched feet of the 50-year-old lady in jeans and T-shirt, for blessing. He wanted a blessing before she managed to cut-off his head for being everywhere in her daughter's life i.e. from her dreams, talks, thoughts, work, plans of movement, that to every time. She murmured may God bless you a long life (Jeetey Raho).

This was the first time, when Kanisk managed to ignore the Purple Lady. He was trying to win a pinch of respect in the eyes of his future mother-in-law.

He tried his best to behave like a decent guy.

Meanwhile, someone was ready to host new problems, and she was her new roomy, Angel, who was known to

Kanisk since a long-time. The girl loved the Purple Lady the way Kanisk loved her, but the intentions of the duo, Kanisk and Angle was different.

Kanisk's intention was to take her away from everyone, get married & live the long life with happiness, where he was able to pray for her. On the other hand, this girl, unaware of our affair and the love platelets flowing in the blood of the duo, she was hunting for some new guy or a life partner for her.

Kanisk asked Angel to accompany Purple's Mom because I felt that she was not happy with my presence.

While, the group was heading towards a mall to buy materials of necessity, the Purple Lady caught Kanisk's hand and slowed him creating gap of few steps from Mom and Angel. While, Angel and Mom were moving ahead, the back-benchers started their romance on the street of Gurgaon, the romance of pinches and pushes followed with few air-born kisses.

Yes it was a pleasing moment for the duo as they were indirectly romancing on the streets that to behind those who would have killed them in a moment if they come to know that the two were in love.

Later, Kanisk tried to be Robin Hood for his mother-in-law in the mall and helped her to remember the things which were necessary for Purple Lady in the new city. Truly saying, she enjoyed Kanisk in Robin Hood format.

By the time, the purchase ended and they moved ahead to the billing counter, Angle and Kanisk entered a debate related to business opportunities in the field of Event Management. Being a business lady, mom entered the discussion and tapped Kanisk's shoulder for his ideas and opinion.

He took the tap as a buzz to the choked heart.

He enjoyed this mode of my life, because he was able to be a collie for his love and secondly for being able to able to impress the lady, who will be his mother-in-law in recent future.

Kanisk wanted to reveal the truth of his love for the Purple Lady, but her eyes stopped him from going ahead.

By now, they were at the PG gate and seeking permission for departure, Kanisk touched the feet of Purple's Mom. He wanted to hug his love, but the scene never happened as she was accompanied with her mother.

Midst this scene of departure, Kanisk managed to hand over some money to Purple Lady that was need of the hour.

He loved the small meet and trillion questions that were carried in the eyes of the Purple Lady.

To be true, his blush and red cheek helped co-passengers in the metro to feel that something is wrong with the guy. Yes, they were right as he was able to smell love after a long interval full of loneliness and solidarity.

Departure of Ma and Kanisk's plans to Move On

After all, the day of departure of Kanisk's mom came, which means regular meets can be done that to without any fear.

Today, Kanisk left the office on time and rushed to her place. They met with Angel as an additional Stepney. None of them hated her but at times her presence can be termed as irritating as in her presence they were not able to communicate or discuss the future aspects of their life, like - when to marry and where to settle down.

They had a dream to die on the same day and the same time, because it was hard for them to live on this earth without the other.

Being aware of the recent monetary problem of the Purple Lady, Kanisk was trying to save every penny that he can to ensure that she may not face some troubles, when he proceeds to his city in Bihar for the marriage of his sister.

Before returning back from Gurgaon, they hurried back to the PG of the lady. At the gate, Kanisk asked Angel to get some water for him with a plan to get a hug from the Purple Lady. Her absence for few minutes helped the duo to hug each other and share few moments of love and internal connection.

By the time of arrival of Angel, Kanisk took a leave from his love and moved on to his place.

This incoming to Gurgaon and departure to his place back turned up to be a daily chorus in Kanisk's life.

Finally the evening came, when Kanisk was supposed to meet her for the last time before being back to home for sister's marriage. T

Today was the day, when she informed him about a guy from his present office who proposed her few days back after they shared Choco Lava with each other at an official function.

He was hurt and she seemed to be happy.

Amid all these disappointments, he finally informed her about his departure from the city and visit to his home town. He also informed her that finally the time has arrived when he will be able to discuss about the lady with his family members.

She urged to wait for few more days before landing into any such discussion but Kanisk was in no mood to hear her plead and said don't worry now I am set to take you to home for lifetime, which means the love birds had an opportunity to settle down after a love relation of 1 year and 11 months.

Smiling and ignoring her comments, he hugged her tight with care of love, and murmured in her right ear, soon after my return will head to your place and ask you hand from your parents.

Her reply was, do you think that they will let a Bihar to do so.

Jokingly he said, if it's my future, I am ready to be shot for her.

Bidding a good bye, he asked her to go back and stood at the PG gate till her disappearance from his sight. Tears were crawling down from his eyes.

They were the tears of love and happiness because he felt that soon she will be legally declared to be his wife. The tears also carried pain of being far from her for few days.

You can say, like every time, these tears were a mix and match of every emotion that he had and any normal human can have.

On being back to the home, he came to know that he failed in give the cheque that he carried to help her with some mney that she may needed in his absence. But he chuckled, as this gave him an opportunity to meet her once again. May be on the day of his departure, I would have met her once again.

Next day, Monday 3rd December 2012, he went early to the office to complete his shift hours. Before leaving for his home, he called her and asked for a meet. She informed that she was on an off from the office and thus she was available for the same.

They met and Kanisk handed her some cash and a cheque along with a debit card. Reminding her to take care of herself and health, he left for the train. But his behaviour this time seemed as if he was staying and the she was about to leave the city.

While bidding me goodbye, she said she will wait for his return and be in continuous touch.

He reached home, took belongings, locked it and took an auto to reach the Railway station. Finally, he was at the station at 7:30 (10 minutes before the scheduled departure).

Ranchi, Marriage and talks related to Purple Lady

Finally, Kanisk was in his city, the city where he spent 15-years of his life as a toddler, child and teen.

Yes, he enjoyed his journey. The marriage was scheduled for 9th December 2012 and he reached the city on 6th December 2012.

Although, it was a time when he was supposed to be on toes to make sure that every arrangement goes in accordance to the plan, he managed to call his love at Gurgaon and shared few words of preparation and family.

After few words of love and togetherness, they engaged in their works.

It was evening, when Kanisk received call of her love informing that her salary from the previous company was transferred at his account ad he needed to deposit the same in her account at the earliest.

He agreed to do so. Taking a leave from his family members for few hours on Saturday when banks function till 12pm. He went to the bank where he was informed link failure will not allow him to deposit the money. This meant that the he will have to wait for two more days, so that he can deposit the money on Monday.

He called her to inform the reason that the money was not deposited due to some technical problem in the bank.

On the other hand, she was shouting that this sorry is not going to change my situation. You can't understand the problem at my end. I have never seen an irresponsible person like you in my lifetime!!!

And the phone hangs on.

He was surprised by the tone and words, which were harsh. After the communication, his conscious and sub-conscious mind entered into a fight. They were arguing, one said are you a servant to her, who keeps nodding his head on all her direction, the other said that no its not so.

After a long fight between the two minds, he managed to call her back to talk. Receiving the phone, she shouted aren't you ashamed? How you dared to call me back?

He replied; don't think that your behaviour is not a good one. People even don't behave in the way to a beggar, the way you are behaving with me.

She said, it was nothing, have you ever imagined.

Imagined what? I think I will have to decide things on you and will have to talk about this incidence when I am back to Delhi.

By the way, I called just to inform that I am going to ask some of my friend to lend some money to you which will be returned by me. Will that work for you?

I want my money, and am not begging to you. He hanged the phone.

This was the worst day of Kanisk's love life or you can term it to be the worst of all the days, he spent on this earth.

On being back, the gentleman who left him on the way to procure some goods required for the marriage enquired Kanisk was the work done. He informed no, there was a problem with the bank and the work can be done only on Monday.

Further, He managed to engage himself with preparations of the marriage.

After two days, the marriage was over and his time to be back to Delhi approached. Till this time, the love birds didn't have any talk.

Kanisk managed to convince himself and called her back.

After two days, he was back to Delhi and fixed a meeting after the office hours.

And it was for Ashu

I was full of hope; my expectation from the unforeseen future, which was just nearer, was something different; I was in a different world all through the day; I was little disturbed and little edgy; still I was holding on to my fort, with butterflies in my tummy. The day passed off as usual in the office and the evening came and my heart beat a little faster.

I was going to meet her. I was going to tell her many things, like, the good news of my sister's marriage; the good news of my discussion I held regarding her with my family and their reaction; the good news of my dream about our life where she was the pivot. I purchased sweets for her.

From the metro I called her and she gave me her new address at Delhi, the hostel (PG) where she was staying. Once there I again called her and after a while she was standing before me.

I kept staring at her and none of us spoke for a while. Finally I handed over the pack of sweets that I brought for her. I looked at her with hope in my eyes.

She did not say anything for a while but when she said I saw pieces of my hope scattered on the floor all across. The resembled like broken glasses to me, with myriads of rainbow staring at me. I was not sure what to do, whether to gather the scattered hopes asking for air like fishes out of water or to take care of, but what to take care. With my hopes shattered there was hardly anything left for me.

I was left alone in our relation, because, I had no place left there as someone else, Ashu-an old acquaintance of her, had entered very swiftly. She was saying she was thankful to me for all that I did for her, as if my role was restricted to being a Good Samaritan. Now, with her problems apparently over she moved on so I must move on, that was what she suggested to me very casually.

Yes! I must move on to the next stage, because there was no space left for me in this arrangement.

For a while I was disconnected from what was happening around me. I was disconnected from everything. With controlled tears in my eyes, and in a state of disconnected shock, I was wondering about my own status. That was a serious question I was asking myself at the cost of my own self-esteem.

I wanted to know why and without showing any remorse or feeling she said, "I think I am happier with him than you, in other words, he is a better guy."

"I was not better," I asked.

"He is a better person," she repeated to my question. Then she added, "I do not want any further discussion in this regard and thanks for being with me in my long and tumultuous journey, which I cannot forget." Then she said good bye and wanted to leave. I did not want to linger the discussion for long as it was hurting my ego. After all I stood along with her at her hardest times and she just dumped me unnecessary garbage accumulated in a house.

That day I walked all the 30 kilometres from her hostel to back to my room. Perhaps that was written for that day in my fate.

I assured her, no I just informed her that at least there would be no botheration from my side. Then she made a big mistake a cardinal one, as she said, "we can remain as two best friends as I always need you."

I glared at her. And she understood what was going on inside me, and she tried to smile, which remained inside her and could not come out.

"What do you think of me? A piece of garbage dumped in home with the hope of some future use. You may have such feeling or idea but, no, I am not like that. I live a very straightforward life without hardly any chance for deceit or cunning; perhaps I am a misfit in your world because I am stupid. But, I like that because that is the way I am and I am proud of it."

I wanted to tell her these words but I did not because that would have been an insult for me. And I would be the last person to score self-goal in life. She dumped me fine, but, my feeling was it was not my fault as I was always honest and true to the time we shared. It was her folly not mines, so why should I be apologetic to anything. Saying all those words would, I felt, would have been like being apologetic to her. I knew time ahead was going to be tough for me but, I must move on. So I did. We in India believe, "whatever happens with you is in your better interest." If that is the fact, where lies the point to unnecessarily bang my head for a situation on which I had no control. But, I certainly have a control on my side so I must not do that. And I did nothing which would have harmed my self-respect anyway. I thank her for making me more resolute and giving an opportunity to learn how to approach adversities of life with your own perspective.

'Thank you!'

Poetic Kanisk

Now his days are a search of himself and nights are sleepless as dreams troubled him forcing him to be awake.

Following the same race, a night of Christmas approached. Sitting at one corner of the garden of life, Kanisk was thinking about the happenings of past and as a joke waited for a call from the friend – who was not a love to him anymore to wish Christmas.

That night he cried like mad. But no one heard his silent cry and this time no one was there to wipe his tears and provide a lap to rest. No one was there to offer a hug, *Jaadu ka Jhappi*, and explain the cause of this pain in life – neither the love nor the friend.

To be true, this was the first night, when he was crying like a child who is lost in a jungle full of big cats. It was hard for him to make any decision as his decision in past went against his principle, moral values and ethics.

He cried today, not to forget her, but was trying to cheat the sleepless nights. He was hoping that it will allow him to sleep. But the thought never worked.

Driving back to home, Kaanisk, who drank for the first time in life, felt that he was getting out of control and hence stopped the bike. For the first time in his life, he managed to sit on the footpath, this time the fearless biker feared driving.

It was mid-night, thus a police patrolling vehicle came and asked him the reason to sit over there, they asked for his ID proofs to verify my identity. After they were sure that Kanisk is a right guy asked him the reason for being over there during the chilling winter night all alone.

Kanisk explained them that he was not feeling well hence decided to sit and take some rest and feel better.

They offered him a hand and promised to drop at his place, which was ignored. Leaving him behind, they moved.

That chilled night for the first time he remained lost on the roads with no destination to reach – a good experience of his life.

Today is the day, when he decided to move on finally from her promising himself not to fall in love again with someone. He wanted to lead the next segment of life by saving the memories of the same love in the heart to all the levels.

Earlier, he had a different definition for love. He believed that love happens without thinking caste and creed, colour and complexion. It just happens without making things accountable. This happened with a guy who is a resident of Bihar from a Sikhni.

It was an acquaintance that made him fall a prey to the thing that he always was scared off. But it happened, it gave him all the pleasures of life – one can ever dream off - and then also allowed him to feel the pain by succumbing to his own decisions.

Walking on the clouds of serenity he found himself all alone on the paths of life. He tried to fill it with colours but was not able to make it last for a longer period of time, as the colours faded away.

He tried to get out of his solitude and cover it with happiness, but the happiness turned up to be a part-time member of life.

He permitted the life to find out the true colours for her, but she was attacked by the darkness and was unable to find out something for her and fell prey to compromises.

He never was able to get any answer to his questions from the Purple Lady, but her pictures on the Social Networking Sites clearly displayed her new face to him. It seemed that she was quite more excited in the new life that included pubs, discos, big cars and restaurants.

After the break-up he wanted to ask few questions with the Purple Lady.

Whether she moved on with the decision of Ashu because he was much younger than him? Was his big car and money to buy all luxuries of life for her was the reason? Was she much happier with the new guy as compared to the level of happiness that she experienced with him? Was she playing around with his emotions for all these years and used him as a path to find out a better solution?

She never answered him back, to any of the questions asked, her only answer was that his presence via any mean was acting as a catalyst in spoiling her relationship with Ashu and his talks were torturing her to all the extents. She said many more things.

But she never answered to the whys' of Kanisk.

These why's always tried to enquire the reason of her change as soon as he left the city of love.

The best part of this loneliness was that Kanisk decided that he will never blame the girl for her decision for dropping him off.

She always had the freedom to move on, whenever she gets someone better than him. This time she got someone who was better and genuine than Kanisk. He was the person who re-defined the meaning of love, joy and happiness for her, something which was done unknowingly by Kanisk in the past.

At the same time, Kanisk was able to understand that she really needed happiness by all craziest means in life. But he understood the same after a wait of about two and a half year long journey with the lady.

What he concluded was that anyone can win her easily just by throwing few droplets of happiness and create an illusion of the same.

At this point of time, he wanted to thank the Purple Lady for leaving him in solitude, as it helped him to re-identify the true Kanisk in himself.

How does it feels, when you think that you knew a person the most, but the person turns up to be a stranger completely at one point of time...!!!

Your presence in my life was the most precious and vulnerable gifts that I ever had, but am sorry to say that you are no more!!!

Life o dear life kindly tell me, that I don't know,

Life o life tell me, the way that I need to go,

Life please tell me, the path that goes the way, where I need to go,

Tell of the way that I need to choose,

The path that will take me, to the place where I need to go,

The place where I can live the way I want to live,

Guide me to the place where I can listen to my heart,

The place where I can speak of my heart,

The place where I can leave on my own standards,

Tell me the way that I need to choose

The place where I can speak of the things to myself,

The place where I can meet to me,

Tell me the place where I can sing a song of life,

And unhide the dreams that I see,

Tell me the way that will take me to the place,

Where I can live up to my own principles,

Life o life, tell me the way that takes me to my future,

I want to go to the way that leads me to the place,

Where I can see the dreams and turn them into a reality,

I know that once I start walking on the ways of dreams,

Then will not have to wait anywhere for anyone,

Life o life, tell me the way,

Where I should go to live the life on my own principles and live up to my expectations.

You are most open to God, when your heart is wide open, and your mind is settled and worry-free. For most of us, this happens in the presence of our beloved.

Before you my life was good, with you it was the best and after you the life has gone pathetic.

From this experience of Kanisk, I as an author of the book, would like to ask a question from the readers.

Is there no place for emotions in this world that is developing at a fast pace? Or had the race with modernity has hooked people to such a level that love had gone materialistic?

They fall prey to the sacred word love in this arena of fast paced lives and lead a pathetic life after sometime.

Printed in the United States
By Bookmasters